The Tao of Mrs. Wei

poems by
Hilary Tham

PS 3570 .H31837 T36 2002
Tham, Hilary, 1946-
The tao of Mrs. Wei

The Bunny and the Crocodile Press
Washington, DC

Copyright © 2003 Hilary Tham
International Standard Book Number: 0-938572-37-7
Library of Congress Control Number: 2002113111

First edition printed 2002
Printed in the U.S.A.

Published by *The Bunny and the Crocodile Press*

No part of this book may be reproduced without the express permission in writing from the publisher. Address inquiries with SASE to:
The Bunny & the Crocodile Press
c/o The Word Works Distribution
P.O. Box 42164
Washington, DC 20015

Cover: "The Dream of Fish," watercolor on paper
by Hilary Tham

Pen & ink illustrations and calligraphy by Hilary Tham
Typography and book design by Cynthia Comitz, *In Support, Inc.*
Printing by George Klear, *Printing Press, Inc.*

Other Books by Hilary Tham

Paper Boats (poems)
Bad Names for Women (poems)
Tigerbone Wine (poems)
Men & Other Strange Myths (poems and art)
Lane With No Name: Memoirs & Poems of a Malaysian Girlhood
Everything's Tough When You're A Teen (poems and art)
Counting: A Long Poem
Reality Check & Other Travel Poems & Art

Acknowledgements

Grateful acknowledgement is made to the publishers and editors of the following journals, anthologies and my poetry books in which these Mrs. Wei poems or earlier versions appeared. My gratitude to publisher Dr. Donald E. Herdeck, whose faith and mentoring have contributed so much to the progress of my writing. And to the New Room Poets: Nancy Allinson, Mel Belin, Dean Blehert, Doris Brody, James Hopkins, Judith McCombs, and Miles David Moore, whose friendship, enthusiasm and demanding critical standards for Mrs. Wei poems helped greatly in the making of many of these poems.

Michael J. Bugeja: *The Art and Craft of Poetry,* Writers Digest Books, Cincinnati, OH 1994: "Mrs. Wei on Patriotism," "Mrs. Wei Wants to Believe the First Amendment."
Snow Summits in the Sun (anthology): "Mrs. Wei & the Beggar," "Mrs. Wei & the Thief," "Mrs. Wei on the Bus."
Metropolitain: "Mrs. Wei on Heroes and Feet."
Minimus: "Mrs. Wei & the Little Winds," "Mrs. Wei Moves Her Gods to America."
Newsletter Inago: "Mrs. Wei Goes to the Dogs," "Mrs. Wei in America."
Phoebe: "Mrs. Wei & the Thief."
Pig Iron: "Mrs. Wei in America."
Poets On: Complaints: "Mrs. Wei is Appalled."
Potomac Review: "Mrs. Wei Meets the New American Dream," "Mrs. Wei Tells Fatslug," retitled "Mrs. Wei Meets Fatslug."
Rockford Review Tributary: "Mrs. Wei at the 56th Annual Craftsmen's Fair."
Shades of Gray: "Mrs. Wei & Tien An Men, June 4, 1989"
Waterways: "Mrs. Wei Refuses to Bury Her Grandmother," "Mrs. Wei In Peking," retitled "Mrs. Wei at the Summer Palace, Beijing"

From *Paper Boats* by Hilary Tham, Copyright © 1987. Used with permission of Lynne Rienner Publishers, Inc.: "Mr. Wei Has No Respect" retitled "Mrs. Wei Complains," "Mrs. Wei on the Bus," "Mrs. Wei and the Goddess of Latrines," "Mrs. Wei Refuses to Bury Her Grandmother," "Thirteen is Terrible, Mrs. Wei Said," "Mrs. Wei Slaps Her Daughter's Hand," "Mrs. Wei & the Holy Water," "Mrs. Wei & the Basket Spirit" retitled "Mrs. Wei Plays the Basket Spirit Game," "Mrs. Wei & the Beggar," "Mrs. Wei & Modern Marriage," "Mrs. Wei Feeds Her Children," "Mrs. Wei & the Thief." From *Bad Names for Women* by Hilary Tham, copyright © 1989. Used with permission of The Word Works, Inc.: "Mrs. Wei Goes Home to Shensi," "Mrs. Wei in Peking" retitled "Mrs. Wei in Beijing," "Mrs. Wei in America" in sections retitled "Mrs. Wei at the Safeway," "Mrs. Wei Visits Niagara Falls," "Mrs. Wei in the Suburbs," "Mrs. Wei is Unhappy with the Sexual Revolution," "Mrs. Wei Goes to the Dogs," "Mrs. Wei Disagrees with Richard Wilbur," "Mrs. Wei Wants to Believe the First Amendment."

From *Tigerbone Wine* by Hilary Tham, Copyright © 1992: "Mrs. Wei at the 56th Annual Craftsmen's Fair," "Mrs. Wei on Heroes & Feet," "Mrs. Wei on Patriotism," "Mrs. Wei & the Gay Poet," "Mrs. Wei on Stupidity," "Mrs. Wei on Bones," "Mrs. Wei on Cats & Traditions."

From *Men & Other Strange Myths* by Hilary Tham, copyright © 1994. Used with permission of Lynne Rienner Publishers, Inc.: "Mrs. Wei & Tien An Men, June 4, 1989," "Mrs. Wei on Education," "Ancestor Worship" retitled "Mrs. Wei & Ancestor Worship," and "Mrs. Wei Sees a Movie."

This book is made possible in part by a Grant in Poetry from the Virginia Commission for the Arts. I am grateful to the Commission for its continuing support.

Contents

1 On Sex, Gods and Politics

Mrs. Wei & Ancestor Worship	13
Mrs. Wei on the Bus	14
Mrs. Wei Sees a Movie	15
Mrs. Wei Wants to Believe the First Amendment	16
Mrs. Wei on Governments	17
Mrs. Wei Meets the New Improved American Dream	18
Mrs. Wei on Heroes & Feet	19
Mrs. Wei is Unhappy with the Sexual Revolution	20
Mrs. Wei on Patriotism	21
Mrs. Wei Reads the Newspaper	22
Mrs. Wei & Tien An Men, June 4, 1989	23
Mrs. Wei on Osama Bin Ladin, 2002	24
Mrs. Wei on Stupidity	26
Mrs. Wei & the Gay Poet	27
Mrs. Wei the Gambler	28
Mrs. Wei Complains	30
Mrs. Wei on Piety	31
Mrs. Wei on Bones	32
Mrs. Wei Refuses to Bury Her Grandmother	33
Mrs. Wei Plays the Basket Spirit Game	34
Mrs. Wei Gets Some Holy Water	36
Mrs. Wei & the Goddess of Latrines	37
Mrs. Wei Disagrees with Richard Wilbur	38

2 On Food, Family & Household Matters

Mrs. Wei & Modern Marriage	41
Mrs. Wei Meets Fatslug	42
Mrs. Wei & the Thief	43
Mrs. Wei on Chicken Soup	44
Mrs. Wei Goes to the Dogs	46

Mrs. Wei & the Beggar	48
Mrs. Wei at the Safeway	49
Mrs. Wei on Crows	50
Mrs. Wei Goes Home to Shensi	52
Mrs. Wei at the Great Wall	53
Mrs. Wei at the Summer Palace, Beijing	54
Mrs. Wei Goes to the Bathroom	55
Mrs. Wei in the Suburbs	56
Mrs. Wei at the 56th Annual Craftsmen's Fair	57
Thirteen Is Terrible, Mrs. Wei Said	58
Mrs. Wei on Education	60
Mrs. Wei Feeds Her Children	61
Mrs. Wei Slaps Her Daughter's Hand	62
Mrs. Wei on the Little Winds	63
Mrs. Wei Visits Niagara Falls	64
Mrs. Wei Reads a Jewish Joke	65
Mrs. Wei Is Appalled	66
Mrs. Wei on Cats & Traditions	68
Mrs. Wei & the Apple Man	69
Mrs. Wei Moves Her Gods to America	70
Author's Notes	73
About the Author	75

The Tao of Mrs. Wei

1

On Sex, Gods and Politics

MRS. WEI & ANCESTOR WORSHIP

An Englishman is visiting his mother's grave
with flowers. He sees Mrs. Wei
spreading a feast of roast chicken,
moo shu pork, noodles
before her father's grave.
"When's your father coming out
to eat that food?" he asks.
Smiling, Mrs. Wei answers,
"Same time your mother
come to smell flowers."

MRS. WEI ON THE BUS

found a seat thankfully set down her bags.
Hot bodies jostled her: schoolgirls in blue,
women shoppers, salesmen, a Buddhist monk

carrying his alms pouch. A schoolgirl
near him struggled toward the exit.
She stumbled over Mrs. Wei's bags.

Mrs. Wei helped her up. "Why are you
leaving? You just got on. Are you
feeling sick?"

Eyes wide, the girl shook her head.
"No—he—the Monk touched me.
I'll catch the next bus."

Mrs. Wei rose in wrath, hissed to the girl
to watch her bags and began to bellow.
"Lecher! Animal! Reptile in saffron robe!

Secret Eater of Forbidden Meat!
Molesting young girls on buses!
I'll report you to your Abbot,

you vomit on Buddha's face!"
Eyes turned. Heads turned. In silence,
he took the path that opened to the exit.

"Always carry a safety-pin," Mrs. Wei said
to the schoolgirl. "When scum like that
surfaces, stab it in the ass.

That jackal is going to be
a lizard in his next life.
May Lord Buddha have mercy on his soul!"

MRS. WEI SEES A MOVIE

Mrs. Wei is watching *Radio Flyer*
where two little boys build a plane
on their go-cart so the five-year-old can fly
away from the alcoholic stepfather
who beats him up half the time.
The mother's a waitress working double shifts
and she doesn't notice
until Bobby has to be hospitalized.
She throws the man out and swears
it will never happen again. But she softens
and takes the man back when he begs
and promises he will change his ways.
"Aiiyah!" Mrs. Wei cries. "Don't do it!
Don't take him back! Don't you know?
The only thing a man will change
for a woman is the way he smells
if she buys him deodorant."

MRS. WEI WANTS TO BELIEVE THE FIRST AMENDMENT

Mrs. Wei in her daughter's house
in America, is sipping her morning coffee,
enjoying the unfamiliar—tulips, oak trees,
a cardinal at the bird feeder.
Her son-in-law shows her the letter
he's writing to voice his displeasure
with the President of the United States.
Mrs. Wei chokes on her coffee
and sputters: "You want a good death?

That letter telling your President
he is wrong, please don't mail it!
I am so afraid for you. Back home, such
forthrightness will drag you to jail,
your family will have to hide their name.
Or worse, a noose on the rain tree, only the wind
to keep your ghost company. Speaking out
is like flying a kite, a banner for police
to track you down.

In my country, we have learned
to fly kites under the bed."

MRS. WEI ON GOVERNMENTS

In Washington, DC, Mrs. Wei takes a tour
of the Capitol and is impressed.
She tells her daughter:
"Malaysian Government is like the American
price system: take it or leave it.
It's easy enough to leave a dress hanging

on the rack, but a country is not something
you can get up and walk away from. Your Congress
resembles our marketplace: haggling and shouting

until everyone is a little satisfied.
Can we visit a shop where I can talk
the price down? I want to buy a victory.

I need a good fight."

MRS. WEI MEETS THE NEW IMPROVED AMERICAN DREAM

My taxi driver from the airport tells me
he loves America, he is studying to be a lawyer
and plans to become very rich, quick.

The workmen from Salvador, building
the house next door, smile because
"Here is no war, much work, good pay."

Their visiting cousin, Silvio, tells me
he is looking for a woman to marry,
any woman who can get him a green card.

"Better if she is blonde with big breasts," he adds,
holding out his hands to show the size
of his dreams, his hope green as an uncut tree.

MRS. WEI ON HEROES & FEET

That President Kennedy brought other women
to his wife's bed is shocking. I would hit him
with a broom if I were his wife.

That San Diego Town changed Martin Luther King
Street back to Market Street because he stole
ideas from a fellow student and slept around

is silly. We are talking tigers here,
not house cats who like to curl up
by the fire when night comes.

Feet of clay do not change how high
these tall men reached. Heroes have feet
ugly with warts and dirt. Let them rest

with their bodies. Better to remember how
they led a nation's feet to high places.
Eyes that watch the ground never see
the sky, never think flying is possible.

MRS. WEI IS UNHAPPY WITH THE SEXUAL REVOLUTION

Equal pay, yes, of course. Equal sex
I cannot understand. They are throwing away
years and years of women's work.
A hundred thousand nights, perfumed skin,
pale bodies that pleasured the Emperor until
he groaned "Yes," and passed a decree of monogamy.
In the morning, he added a law for concubines.

From the beginning, women have made men pay
for sex—a leg of wild boar, gold
chains, marriage. Now, their daughters
give it away, call it freedom! And the men,
the men are laughing as they go
from bed to bed to bed. A basket of scuttling
crabs let loose while dog bites dog-bone.

MRS. WEI ON PATRIOTISM

Here many people over-exercise
their right to free speech. Everywhere
bumper stickers shout at me: Have you
hugged your child today? I brake
for animals! Honk if you love
Jesus! We support our troops! Say No
to drugs! I am for America!
But when they want us all
to chant slogans and tie yellow
ribbons to our houses, I plant
my feet and say No.

Loyalty to one's land should be
as natural as sap in the tree
whose roots know the earth which gives
it sustenance. It is not a hair ribbon
to run to the store to buy
when it becomes fashionable.

MRS. WEI READS THE NEWSPAPER

I think I understand why dead souls drink
the tea of oblivion before rebirth.
The news of criminals like the man who killed

and froze young boys for future dinners
wrings the blood from my heart.
Lord Buddha, let such be reborn

as worms stranded on roads after rain
to dry and die. Let them be reborn as roaches
we squash with hard-soled sandals and disgust.

I would not waste one tear on their suffering.
Let them learn to be human as they crawl
up the ladder of reincarnation again.

MRS. WEI & TIEN AN MEN, JUNE 4, 1989

Thirty years ago, my China cousins wanted
me to send them cooking oil, their highest hope
was a sewing machine or a bicycle.

Today, their children want something unheard of
in their parents' dreams: they want freedom!
They've dropped their books in university rooms,
they've built a plaster Goddess of Democracy
like the Statue of Liberty in New York harbor.
All week long, the students are chanting
for new, freer laws. Office workers, factory
workers are rushing to join them.
Wedding couples pose for pictures
beside the statue. Look at the little boy
sucking his thumb, smiling because
his grown-ups are happy.
They ignore the summer heat,
the lack of bathrooms,
the stink of body fluids, body waste,
the soiled toilet paper everywhere in the square.
They laugh at the guns and soldiers
surrounding the square.

Oh rash young people, to believe
tigers can be tamed by words.
Didn't your mothers teach you?
You cannot lead tigers
away from the mountain.
Better to wait
till sleeping tigers die of old age.

MRS. WEI ON OSAMA BIN LADEN, 2002

September 11, my friend calls: "Turn on your TV!"
I turn on my TV. Heaven is splitting open,
the earth trembles and thunder pours in my ear.

A thief has entered the house
and grabbed a sword, using America's own planes
to steal the sky and hide the sun.

All I can say is: Here is a rat,
a rat crossing the street
to bite a tiger's tail.

Now precious jade is broken,
yesterday's mirror shattered, and patrolling jets
darken the skies like crows.

MRS. WEI ON STUPIDITY

The first time Mrs. Wei visited America,
her daughter Lan Li showed her how to shower
in an American bathroom.
"You stand inside the tub, Ma," Lan said.
"May's mother filled the tub and poured
water on herself, outside the tub.
She flooded the bathroom."

Mrs. Wei nodded. "Buddha bless me,
the bathroom floor doesn't have a drain?
I would have felt really stupid
flooding your bathroom. I would have
felt as stupid as an engineer
holding a suitcase-bomb and a plane ticket,
or as stupid as a terrorist told to build
a bridge for a big, fierce river."

MRS. WEI & THE GAY POET

He wore an orange silk scarf and jacket.
His denim jeans were tight, with holes
to air his knees. I don't understand this

rage to beat up new clothes with stones
until a beggar would refuse to wear them.
He talked about sex between man and man.

I think sex should be pillow talk, not
shouted from a platform. His poem
asking his mother if he could bring

his husband home to dinner was so sad.
I hope she said yes, poor mother,
the grandchildren she wants, grandchildren

she will never have. She mourns her son,
watching him turn away, take the path
the ancient Greeks took to extinction,

precipice where love carves names on stone,
the single tree wastes itself, seeding
barren rock and the cold salt sea.

MRS. WEI THE GAMBLER

One moonless time I was hungry for money.
I went to the graveyard across the road
to beg lottery numbers from a ghost.

It was scary there, just me and neighbor Long
among the old Chinese grave mounds,
only the wind moving the grass—shush, shush

at us. "How do we know which grave holds
a kindly-disposed gambling ghost?" I whispered,
thinking I should have asked Long these things

in daylight, not shivering by gravestones hoping
for spirits. "We'll know when we bump into it,"
she said, creeping ahead to another grave.

Just then, headlights, cars pulling up, car doors
slamming. "Oh gods protect us, it's the police!
Hide, we've got to hide!" Long dived

into the bushes and I after her. Of course they
were thorn bushes! How those brambles scritched
and scratched at us! It wasn't the police after all,

only that lucky man Sung who won
the lottery last week, with his friends bringing Hell
money, paper mansion, and a whole roast pig

to thank the ghost for giving him lucky numbers.
After they left, Long said, "That is one huge pig!
Let's take a piece for you and me."

"Better to steal from the living," I said
as I dragged her home. "People may hurt your body
but ghosts can drag your soul to Hell."

Later we heard the helpful ghost wanted more
than the roast pig, she wanted Sung for a husband.
He consulted every spiritualist in town but to no avail.

The ghost took him after three months.
Poor Sung! At least his lottery money
got him a splendid funeral.

MRS. WEI COMPLAINS

Mr. Wei has no respect for the gods.
At Ching Ming he steps on graves
and sits on tombstones.

I have to offer apologies and incense
on his behalf to pacify their occupants.
On New Year and all the festivals

when I pray and offer food
to the gods, he shouts
from the dining hall, "Hurry up!

The gods have tasted enough.
The food will get cold.
I'm hungry!"

MRS. WEI ON PIETY

My Buddhist friend, Kim, has arms
dotted with red pinpricks where mosquitoes
have drunk their fill. She's so devout she will kill nothing,

not even a fire ant with its sharp mandibles in her foot.
Flies play tag in her kitchen while she holds the door
open, begs them to leave.

They don't go, they invite other flies in to the feast
of soybeans and tofu in her vegetarian kitchen.
Now, I believe in Lord Buddha, but within reason.

When she offers me food, I shake my head.
Everyone knows flies stomp their feet in dung
before they come into a house.

MRS. WEI ON BONES

When her granddaughter is born, Mrs. Wei
opens her almanac to weigh the baby's bones.
She tells daughter Lan Li: "We Chinese know
our fortunes hang on how heavy our bones are.
Birth at the hour of the Monkey means

half an ounce, the Rooster's year
adds another and a half. Though a body
may sleep on silk and drive in limousines,
feather-weight bones will end poor,
whether it is "Mah sei lohk deih haahng"
(the horse being dead, get down and walk) or

"Dor tew hor paau" (the purse hung upside down).
Bone weight—the sum of birth year, month, day, hour—
binds us all. Beggar bones weigh two ounces,

seven ounces mean the life of a king
or president. Our efforts can change the next life,
can tip a soul into a bone-heavy body.

MRS. WEI REFUSES TO BURY HER GRANDMOTHER

In the Prosperity Hill Cemetery, Mrs. Wei
shakes her head as she is offered one burial plot
after another. "The *feng shui* is no good on that plot,
the slope is bad, the luck will wash away.
This one is too flat—luck will stagnate here.
Burial in such plots will bring sorrow
to the family, poverty, or the birth of daughters.

Grandmother will have to be cremated.
We can keep her ashes on a temple shelf
until a better plot becomes available."

MRS. WEI PLAYS THE BASKET SPIRIT GAME

You put chopsticks through the handles
of a used basket, hang the chopsticks high
on chairs and invite a spirit with incense and cakes.

Basket spirits are usually nice
gossipy women ghosts who help
pass an afternoon pleasantly.

Was Father happy in his new
house in Ghost Village? Did he live
with my mother or his first wife?

Which number will win the lottery?
Is there wealth in my near future?
Does my husband keep a mistress?

Many afternoons I invited
a spirit in to visit. Most were
glad to chat, sometimes a grumpy one

roused from her nap, would come,
rocking short and seldom, wanting
only to leave. No fun at all.

Then one came who refused to leave.
It jumped off its chopstick holder
when I tried to say goodbye.

It was friendly as a puppy
after meat scraps, wobbling after me
as I backed into the kitchen.

Holy Mountains! the idea of life
with a basket at my heels—such
embarrassment! Holy Mountains!

It took an hour of sweet talk
while I lied and sweated before it left.
No more spirit games for me!

MRS. WEI GETS SOME HOLY WATER

We all want to believe in miracles.
When I was young, a rumor ran through our town
of a new healing spring by the railroad.

No one had witnessed its cures
but everyone knew someone who knew
someone who knew someone who had.

We washed and sterilized bottles
and congregated by the railroad
the next day

and the next, slowing down
all the trains. Some profiteers
sold bottles to passengers

as the trains inched by.
Soon everyone in town had a bottle
of holy water for home use. Then

the spring dried up. I suspect
the Railroad Company piped it elsewhere.
Weeks later, I found wrigglers

in my bottle and threw the water out
without testing its powers.
I should have boiled it first.

MRS. WEI & THE GODDESS OF LATRINES

Too much attention embarrasses
the Goddess of Latrines. She's very shy.
That's why no one prays to her anymore.

I remember her at New Year. I burn
a stick of incense by the toilet.
She did me a favor once.

Men Yu, my first-born, was so sickly
his first hundred days of life.
I burnt slippers around his cradle,

put stones in the front door, but
the *thou-tzu* ghosts were not scared.
They were hungry and strong.

Each morning he was sicker, weaker.
My mother said, "Put him in the latrine.
Maybe the Goddess will hide him

from those childless ghosts."
Men Yu stayed in the bathroom
till he passed his hundred days.

Then the *thou tzu* were powerless.
So I remember the Goddess at New Year.
More attention would scare her away.

MRS. WEI DISAGREES WITH RICHARD WILBUR

> *"The snow came down last night like moths burned on the Moon."*
> — Richard Wilbur

No, no, it's the Lady-in-the-Moon
doing her laundry, though, living alone, what
has she got to wash? I know, she's cutting
her white rabbit's hair.
Sometimes I worry, she must be bored,
so many centuries on the same old moon,
not even a change of furniture. I guess
the first hundred years she was glad
to escape that bragging, wine-swilling
hero husband of hers, but immortality
without family or friends is to dine on snow,
like too-long immersion in stale bath water,
tedious till painful. Centuries of nothing
except for the astronauts' visit.
Anything is bearable if you know it is temporary.
Tonight I shall offer incense, tell her
there is talk of a moon station.

2

On Food, Family & Household Matters

MRS. WEI & MODERN MARRIAGE

Nowadays people are more romantic;
they kiss and cuddle even after
marriage. It looks very nice.

The men of my generation
kiss only low women. Couples
are water buffalo in a plow.

Now plows are easily dropped,
the buffalo run wild after kissing
while we stay in our fields.

Mr. Wei and I have never kissed.
Luckily he is more interested
in high cuisine than low women.

MRS. WEI MEETS FATSLUG

My dear boy, never mind dieting!
You must change your name.
Such an unlucky name entraps

the spirit, attracts hungry ghosts.
They'll move in. You will eat and eat
and never fill their stomachs.

Good things come to a good name,
even love, which gods know, is a picky phoenix
wanting *handsome*, inside and out.

Be glad, as the laughing Buddha, to be
alive and that suicidal bird will come to your hand.
Even the gods love *sunny*, love *tasty*.

Don't salt your meals with guilt. The tangiest
General Tso's chicken isn't good eating in the grave.
And that's a trap no one escapes.

MRS. WEI & THE THIEF

When I heard the rooster scream,
the hens in noisy panic, I knew
a thief was in my chicken house.

Grabbing a flashlight and a rattan cane
I ran to see a six-foot cobra,
patterned like woven grass, leave

with my best layer in its mouth.
It flowed swift as running water
into the cemetery behind the shed.

I followed, jumping over graves.
"Excuse me, please excuse," I said
to placate any ghosts about to rise.

I caught up to that jeweled spatula-head,
flailed it with my cane until
its gleaming eyes dulled,

then dragged its limpness to the road,
and stretched it out to be killed again,
its bright green pounded black

by passing cars, the sure way to kill
snake magic. Then I took my chicken
home for dinner.

MRS. WEI ON CHICKEN SOUP

I used to keep a rooster with my chickens. Its crokooroo
crowing chased away night demons. But I never kept it long.
My husband's mother loved rooster meat,

she thought it would prolong her life.
Soon as the rooster grew big enough to have meat,
she would take to her bed with moans and groans,

claim she was dying. After three days of her moaning,
I'd give in and kill the young rooster, simmer it
with *dong kwai* and herbs for her dinner.

A rooster was a small enough price to pay for peace
and quiet in the house. Myself, I prefer the sweeter
meat of chicken in soup, not that we could afford it.

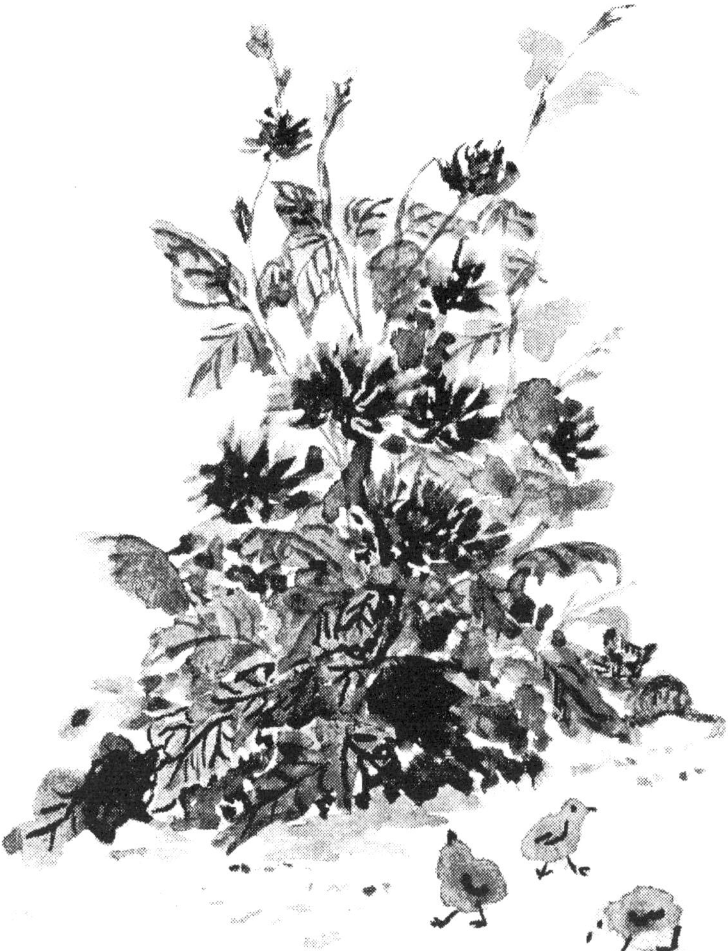

MRS. WEI GOES TO THE DOGS

We Chinese have no use for dogs
except as health food to heat the blood
like vitamin E or rhino horn.

A flock of geese, their wings raised
like shields, snakeheads, a stabbing of spears,
make better house guards.

Cormorants pay for their board with fish.
My cat earns his place. The day I find
mice in my kitchen, out he goes.

Some people claim a mongrel that chooses
their home brings luck. That must be
why I keep feeding this useless mutt.

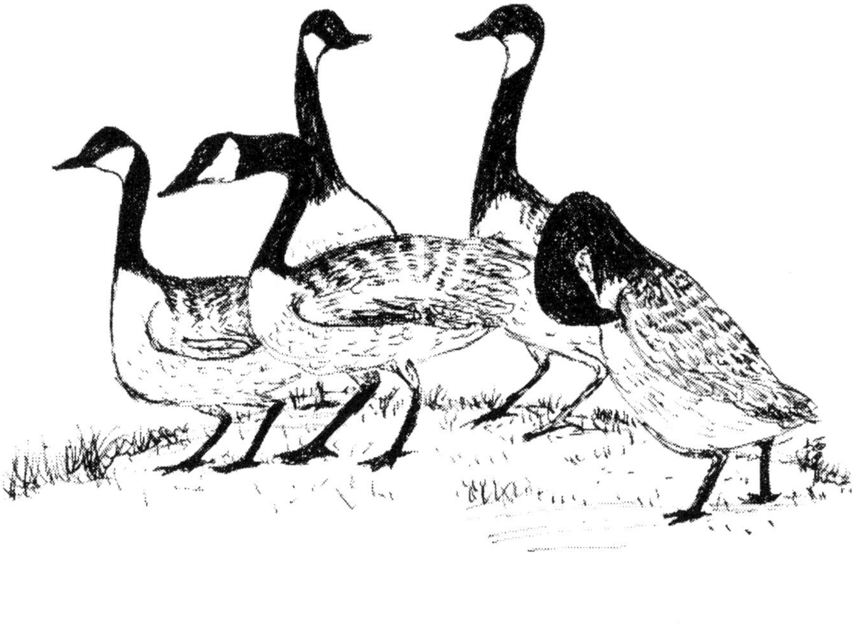

MRS. WEI & THE BEGGAR

Sunday morning filled with quiet
and sleepers, this beggar rattles
his tin cup at our gate.

He is tall, once had muscles,
his eyes are stained
with opium yellow.

I put ten cents in his cup
feeling kind on this gentle day.
He picks it out and spits at it

and me. The nerve, when twenty buys
a meal of hot noodles,
a half-loaf of bread

with a paper of jam to go.
He curses me for mocking
a sick man

calls on gods in earth and sky
to ill-gift me and mine.
He makes such a din banging

his dented cup on my wrought-iron gate
I consider turning
the garden hose on him.

He makes such a din he wakes
Mr. Wei, who erupts from the house
in red pajamas and a black face

and spews hot curses like a volcano.
As he runs from Mr. Wei, that beggar
looks very healthy.

MRS. WEI AT THE SAFEWAY

Used to shopping in wet markets where the butcher
would slap her chosen cut of meat on a page
of newspaper, roll it up and tie it with string,
Mrs. Wei is dazzled in the supermarket, wanders
the aisles like Alice in Wonderland. "Aiiyah," she whispers
to her daughter, "American food is beautiful.
Such pretty wrapping, so many colors!
The clever shapes of glass and plastic.

I want to take these containers home
to Malaysia, impress my neighbors.
Too bad American meat has no smell.
The water, too, tastes strange, even after boiling.
I'll be glad to be home where foods smell right
and I can argue with the butcher, get an extra
ounce by calling him Miser."

MRS. WEI ON CROWS

The black crow has an evil voice
but a good heart. Young crows care
for their parents when they are old

or sick. They bring food in their beaks
from miles and miles away
for parent crows to eat.

Crows can see and hear the dead.
That's why they sit for hours in cemeteries,
shifting from branch to branch, talking

to the whispering air around them. It's bad luck
to hear a crow jeering ill-wishes, "Ngah, ngah—
teeth, teeth" early in the morning.

Bad joss for weddings, business beginnings—
rough winds and heavy rain will break
the green stalks in your young rice field.

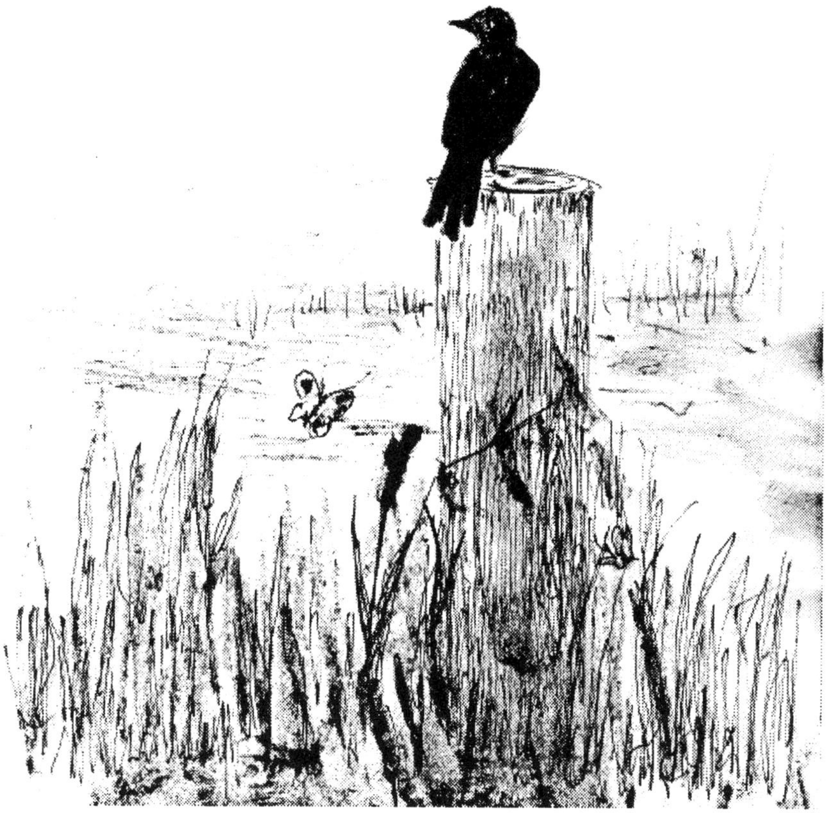

MRS. WEI GOES HOME TO SHENSI

Aiiyah... they told me, they told me true.
See Shanghai, Beijing, XiAn first, but I
would not listen. Ancestral village, then

the tours. I never dreamed a family
so extended, so devoted.
They trudge for miles, hitch rides

on two-horse-power tractors, pony carts,
arrive begrimed with road dust
just to see my face. My traveler's checks

vanish like dew on late morning grass,
exchanged for *yuan*, sacks of rice.
"You must stay to dinner

(and breakfast) before your trip home."
My uncle's wife's brother-in-law
says he rises at five to work the commune farm,

at dark returns to hoe his ginger patch.
It brings in *fen* for thread and cloth.
We serve no banquet, no salted radish either.

Sun-darkened, sinewy, they gulp
tureens of rice, ask about the legendary
Nanyang gold! Cousin Shiao Lin introduces

the fifth son-in-law of my grandmother's
third cousin. And his family. She whispers, "We need
to buy more food." I forage in my purse,

regret I won't see Shanghai. I must leave
before the money for Beijing goes.
XiAn went for eighty cousins yesterday.

MRS. WEI AT THE GREAT WALL

All my life I've wanted to see this
Ten Thousand Li Great Wall.
Now I am sixty-five, too old for change

and Communism, the Malaysian Visa Office
permits I visit the land of my ancestors.
Oh, my arthritic knees! This wall was built

for mountain goats! The Emperor's soldiers
perched on the edge of the world, wanting
to sow rice and children, making do

with mulled wine against snow and ghost voices
wailing in the stones. Poor dead soldiers—
their breaths chill the stone, the summer wind.
I feel it. This Wall is haunted.

MRS. WEI AT THE SUMMER PALACE, BEIJING

So this is the Summer Palace! The guide says
this lake was dug by thousands with shovels.
The Dowager Empress was vain: mirrors

line her pavilions! I can't eat
our banquet of her favorite foods. I've tasted
better in Singapore, San Francisco, Taipei.

The guide says she insisted on one hundred
twenty courses for dinner. With her bound feet,
no exercise. No wonder she grew fat.

Did she eat to forget she poisoned her son?
I wonder where in all this splendor
the bathroom is hidden?

MRS. WEI GOES TO THE BATHROOM

Now I'm not fussy about latrines.
I pack toilet paper in my purse,
and know well the *Honeyman*'s scents.

But latrines with doors of air,
exposed as a newborn snail. *Aiiyah!*
This is too bare for me. But after all,

the woman in the opposite stall knows
there's nothing new to see. I'll squat
as she does, turn my eyes to the wall.

MRS. WEI IN THE SUBURBS

Mrs. Wei is pretending to watch television
in her daughter's living room. She keeps an eye
on the huge picture window and the garden.
She keeps a hand on the rolling pin in her lap.
She relaxes when she hears her daughter come in.
"Hi Ma, I'm home," Lan Li says, and stares
at the rolling pin in her mother's hand.
"What's that for?"

"To hit the burglar on the head," Mrs. Wei
says, unabashed. "American architects are just
too trusting. Ants bite my heart when I am alone
in your house. Picture windows invite thieves.
Malaysian houses are safer. Padlocked iron gates,
barred windows, broken glass on wall ledges
keep robbers and salesmen at a respectful distance.
I don't feel safe here."

MRS. WEI AT THE 56TH ANNUAL CRAFTSMEN'S FAIR

Buddha bless my eyes! Four hundred dollars
for a hand-knitted dress. Woolworth's or Penney's
could cover ten naked bodies for less.

This quilted bib is lovely; but
ten dollars for something the baby
will dribble and spit up spinach on?

Why is America walking backwards?
That woman slapping, shaping clay
this long hot day to make a dinosaur

water jug that will whistle a tune
for show, leaking water all the while—
better she should be making babies!

THIRTEEN IS TERRIBLE, MRS. WEI SAID

It took four miracles, one per
child, to raise my first four
past that unlucky age.

Each had to be hospitalized
during the thirteenth year:
Men Yu for jaundice, his skin turned

yellow as a monk's saffron robe.
Then Lan Li got under a pot
of boiling water. They peeled

the puffed skin off her legs
at the hospital. I swore I'd never
say "I'll skin you alive" again.

Then the mysterious sickness
that made Men Ya swell and swell.
The doctors were shaking their heads.

I went to Kuan Yin's temple.
The medium said Third Grandaunt's ghost
wanted his soul to keep her company.

So I took a stone from her grave
saying "I reclaim what belongs
to me." Men Ya recovered

after he drank the soup I made
with that stone. I burnt a paper doll,
a boy, to keep Grandaunt happy.

When Lan Fa had pneumonia
at thirteen, I realized the presence
of the Thirteenth Doorway Demons.

I promised Kuan Yin a roast
suckling pig, gold and silver
for her protection against them.

After that, none of the other
children had problems. If I had known
sooner, I'd have had fewer nights of fear.

MRS. WEI ON EDUCATION

The Wong family next door had a daughter
they refused to send to school though Kim begged
to go with my daughters.

"Sons need education for earning power,
Old Wong told me, "but a girl only needs pretty
dresses and a good matchmaker like me."

Old Wong ran around town making matches
while collecting laundry for his wife
and daughter to wash and iron.

He never made a connection for his daughter.
She ran away to Singapore and found
her own man to marry.

As the sapling is bent, so grows the tree.
Today Kim says her father was right.
Luckily, she only has sons.

MRS. WEI FEEDS HER CHILDREN

When Mrs. Wei heard American mothers got
their children to eat by telling them people
were starving in Poland, she laughed.
"That wouldn't have worked for us—
in Malaysia, people were starving in our town.
I told my children the same things my mother
told me: Eat your rice, watch your chopstick hand,
keep your palm up. Never turn the back
of your hand to Heaven, the gods
will mark you for rebellious thoughts.

And if they left the table with rice in their bowl,
I'd say: Come back! You left ten grains of rice
in your bowl. You'll offend the God of Planting.
Do you want to put pockmarks on the face
of your future wife? It worked.
They cleaned their bowls."

MRS. WEI SLAPS HER DAUGHTER'S HAND

Don't throw that string away!
It can still be used.
Your dead grandfather, the scholar,
always said: By the river,
don't waste water. By the forest,
don't waste wood.
The Earth gods watch their gifts.
They take them back from wastrels.

He also said: Wealth will not last
three generations in one family.
The first grabs it, the second
saves it, the third spends it.
Look at the Lu family.

Old Mr. Lu still rides
his creaky bicycle to his shop.
His grandsons go in chauffeured cars.
Their children will walk to
bus-stops and envy others.
The gleam of gold fades
from Ancestor Lu's bones,
it rises in another's.

MRS. WEI ON THE LITTLE WINDS

When the little winds blow the fallen leaves
into spinning circles I know the spirits
of mischief are about. I tell the children:

Don't stare at the little winds.
They could take offence and slap your face
into a snarl that would send you
into a permanent dance with doctors.

My second aunt forgot to warn her daughter
about the little winds. My poor cousin laughed
and pointed, once, at a spinning circle of leaves.

All the doctors of medicine, East and West,
could not return her sense of smell or straighten
her nose from pointing at her right ear.

MRS. WEI VISITS NIAGARA FALLS

What a big falling of water, what a hugeness
of land. No wonder Americans like everything bigger.

Everything here is big, especially the roads.
I like it that cars and their drivers are polite.
Back home, eight tiger cars would have squeezed

into the space between this car and the next,
their drivers giving you the finger
for tamely waiting in line.

MRS. WEI READS A JEWISH JOKE

We Chinese laugh at slapstick, love
the Three Stooges, are confused by strange
play of words that tickle others.

I am reading this joke about a professor
at an international school. He tells the class
to write a paper on the Elephant.

The student from Germany hands in "A Bibliography
of Books on Elephants," the French student: "Love
Among the Elephants," the English student: "Elephant Hunting,"

the American student: "How to Breed Bigger and Better
Elephants," and the Jewish student: "The Elephant
and the Jewish Problem."

I am thinking: if this class had a Chinese student,
he would write "99 Ways to Cook Elephant Meat."
We Chinese have known famine time after time,

we have found ways to cook anything, tree fungus,
anteater, sea slugs. The harder part is to sell it
to the squeamish of stomach. You have to invent

reasons for people to swallow these things;
say it works like Viagra and is more organic.
Then charge a high price.

In Beijing, my friends took me to the Duck Palace,
ordered the most expensive dishes: duck feet,
duck heart, duck tongue, duck skin.

I had a hollow feeling in my gut; the cooks
must laugh at us fools as they smack their lips
on meaty breasts and drumsticks.

MRS. WEI IS APPALLED

When Mrs. Wei sees her Singapore daughter
feeding imported cans of pet food: tuna, liver,
chicken to her cats, she shakes her head,
keeps her thoughts behind her teeth: *Those strays
eat better than a lot of people I know.*

But when the daughter in America pays the vet
a hundred dollars for her cat to have its teeth
cleaned, it is more than a mother can bear.
"Buddha bless us—that cat will be disappointed
when he gets reborn as a human, he'll think
he's really come down in the world."

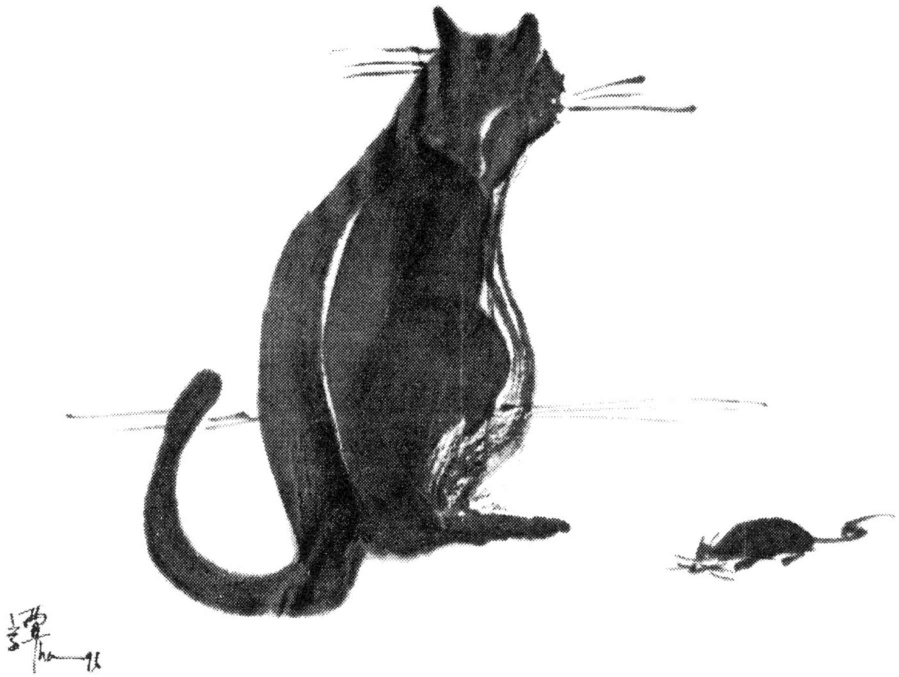

MRS. WEI ON CATS & TRADITIONS

Traditions are good to have. Like gods,
they help furnish our children's hearts.
A child in an empty room must fill it,
if only with the sound of his voice crying.

But too many traditions or gods
can be bad. When you bring them home,
they stay forever. You end up like
the woman with twenty-nine cats,
keeping them, cooking for them,
cleaning litter boxes long after
the children have left home.

MRS. WEI & THE APPLE MAN

The most stubborn man I know
is that man from Surabaya who
planted an apple orchard

among sugarcanes and bananas.
His trees grew pretty and green but
would not bear fruit without the cold

and wintering. For the fruit he loves,
he pays women and children
to pick off every leaf in October.

When I think of all the different
tasty apples he could have imported
from Australia, England, America,

I can only say, What a cow's head!

MRS. WEI MOVES HER GODS TO AMERICA

Mrs. Wei carefully rolled her porcelain Buddha
in tissue paper and bubble wrap and laid the bundle
gently in her little suitcase. She did the same to Kuan-yin,
Goddess of Mercy, adding towels for extra cushioning.
She wasn't too worried—saying, "They're gods,
they should be able to protect themselves.
I told them I'd have a new altar for them
soon as I can. I had to burn the old altar to ash
so it shouldn't be profaned by a disbeliever.

When I die, (my daughters say *Don't talk about that*,
but I tell them, *Life is a loan, don't
take it for granted. If I'm lucky, I'll die well.
If not, not.*) just tell the gods I'm gone and it's time
for them to leave. Keep the statues as curios.

I hope Buddha and Kuan-yin will like America.
I like America—old people are more alive here,
they don't sit themselves on a dusty shelf
to eat, sleep and wait for death; they take classes
in poetry or movie-making. I love my painting
class. Maybe the gods could use a hobby too."

Double Happiness

Author's Note

I first came across the concept of "the Jewish Mother" and "the Italian Mother" when I came to America after my marriage. This set my mind to wondering what were the main characteristics of Chinese mothers in general. Chinese girls were raised to be gentle, docile, submissive to husbands and elders. We were told we could become powerful and speak out only when we had become mothers of sons and had reached sixty: the age of wisdom.

I observed this phenomenon of Chinese women suddenly becoming forceful and opinionated when they became matriarchs. Most of the Chinese mothers I knew, including my own, were raised with very little education, as education was considered not necessary for girls. However, they became home-grown philosophers gathering their wisdom from life and practical application of truths their observation and experience gained them. I believe my Mrs. Wei sprang from an amalgamation of my mother and the mothers of my friends and the side of myself that wanted to shout at the world sometimes.

My first Mrs. Wei poem was "Mrs. Wei on the Bus." I asked myself what would the quintessential Chinese Mother do confronted with such a situation as had occurred to me and a friend on a bus when we were in our teens. And thus Mrs. Wei sprang full grown and vociferous into existence. To my surprise, Mrs. Wei captured the hearts of many of my readers and even very politically correct readers express enjoyment of her vehement "fishwife" takes on modern issues.

More Mrs. Wei poems came as I found the persona of an older, wiser, respected-for-her-age woman a useful vehicle to craft my poems in response to many facets of society. As I aged and grew more confident in my right to speak my opinion in my own voice, I have written less Mrs. Wei poems. I am grateful for the gifts of the poems she gave me. From her, I learned the courage to speak out for myself.

— Hilary Tham

About the Author

Hilary Tham, of Arlington, Virginia, is an artist and author of seven books of poetry, and a memoir: *Lane With No Name.* Her poetry and short fiction have been published in the USA, Malaysia, New Zealand, and translated into Hebrew in Israel and Chinese in Taiwan. She has been a tutor to Malaysian princesses and holds a B.A. (Hons) in English Literature from the University of Malaya, Malaysia. Her work is studied in Malaysia as a major woman poet in the corpus of Malaysian Literature in English. She teaches creative writing and has been awarded many Artist-in-Education grants and a Poetry fellowship from the Virginia Commission for the Arts. She is editor-in-chief for the Word Works and poetry editor for Potomac Review, where she also writes a regular column, "Poetic Justice."